First published in the United States, Great Britain, Canada, Australia, and New
Zealand in 2013 by NorthSouth Books, Inc., an imprint of NordSüd Verlag AG,
CH-8005 Zürich, Switzerland.

Distributed in the United States by NorthSouth Books Inc., New York 10016.
Library of Congress Cataloging-in-Publication Data is available.

ISBN: 978-0-7358-4117-8 (trade edition)
Printed in Germany by Grafisches Centrum Cuno GmbH & Co. KG, 39240 Calbe,
April 2013.
1 3 5 7 9 • 10 8 6 4 2
www.northsouth.com

Will You Be My Friend?

BERNADETTE WATTS

North South

In the morning, when Little Jack Rabbit put his nose outside, the whole world was glittering with frost. *Brr!* It was bitterly cold.

In the afternoon the sun fell behind the hill long before suppertime. Then, when it got dark and the wintry wind whined, Little Jack's father put a rug against the door to keep out the draft.

"Tomorrow," he said, "we will go to the cabbage field."

Early the next day, the whole family and some neighbors took the long journey across the field, through the hedge, around the hill, and into another field. And there were the juicy cabbages, in long rows, all looked after by a scarecrow.

"Don't mind him," said Father. "He can't walk. He only has one leg."

"And he does not speak our language," added an uncle.

"He has got a horrid yellow face and horrid red paws," said an aunt, "and no ears at all. He is not one of us."

"He has got kind eyes," said Little Jack.

"And that means he has a warm heart," said his mother.

The day was short. The light faded. It got cold. The rabbits started for home.

The scarecrow felt sad to see the rabbits leave. He wondered if they would return. All next day, and the day after, he watched for them. He was lonely, stuck in the middle of the field on one wooden leg.

The nights grew colder, and the stars shone brighter. The days got shorter, and the earth got harder. The flowers and grasses went underground to sleep until next spring.

Little Jack Rabbit ran to the tree where Billy Squirrel lived.

"Would you like to come to the cabbage field?" he asked Billy.

Little Jack admired Billy because Billy was brave enough to climb trees, and he thought it was a good idea to take him along.

Billy's parents were extremely busy and did not notice them leave.

Halfway across the field they came to the Moles' house.

"Oh, can I come too?" cried Little Charlie Mole. And he ran along behind Jack and Billy as fast as his little legs would go.

Suddenly they met an old hare.

"Where are you going?" asked the hare.

"Only to the cabbage field," replied Little Jack.

The hare twitched his long ears and said, "Well, make sure you go home before dark." And he watched them trot off across the field.

"Don't be afraid of the scarecrow," said Little
Jack Rabbit.

"I'm not afraid of a scarecrow!" said Billy Squirrel.

"I am," whispered Little Charlie Mole.

"He can't chase you, "said Little Jack. "He only
has one leg."

"Has he been in a trap?" asked Little Charlie,
trembling.

"Oh, let's eat some cabbages!" said Billy.

They ate all day. Then the evening clouds gathered, and a chilly wind sprang up.

"I want to go home," said Little Charlie Mole.

The wind ran around and made strange noises among the cabbages.

"I want to go home," said Little Charlie.

Suddenly it was very dark. The animals were not sure of their way home.

Then the first flakes of snow fluttered down.

Little Jack looked up for the moon and the stars, but there was only the dark and the whirling snow. He looked at the scarecrow. How the wind tugged at his gloves and tore at his coat!

Suddenly the scarecrow lurched forward, and the feather jumped out of his hat.

Little Charlie trembled and held on to Little Jack's paw. "I WANT TO GO HOME NOW!" he cried.

But Little Jack said, "We cannot go home till morning."

"We must find shelter," added Billy.

He hopped up to the scarecrow, and Little Jack Rabbit and Little Charlie Mole followed behind. They crouched close to the scarecrow's leg.

The scarecrow leaned over as if he wanted to say something.

The night got darker. The wind blew wilder. The snow fell thicker.

The scarecrow lost one of his gloves, and his hat was tossed away. He leaned again, flapping his arms.

Billy, Jack, and Charlie clung to one another, shivering.

Then the scarecrow lay down next to them and with one arm wrapped his coat around them. Then with his other arm he cuddled his new friends close to his heart.

"I'm really warm now," said Billy, snuggling down.

"Thank you, Mr. Scarecrow," said Charlie. Then he squeezed his eyes tight and fell asleep.

Little Jack Rabbit looked up at the scarecrow's face and saw tears in his eyes. He touched the scarecrow's cheek and felt that it was wet.

All night the wind whistled across the lonely field. Little Jack Rabbit thought of home.

The next morning the snow lay deep
for as far as you could see. The wind had
dropped. The whole world was still.

Little Jack Rabbit peeped out. Now the
sun was coming up. The golden light spilled
through the trees and hedges, over the farm
roof, and across the white field. Suddenly, the
sky was bright blue.

"Wake up! Wake up!" shouted Little Jack.
Little Charlie scrambled outside, sniffing the air.
"I can smell my home! It's over there!" he cried,
pointing toward the hill.

The three friends set off for home. They tumbled through snowdrifts, and Little Charlie fell over several times.

They pushed through the snow-laden hedge.
"This is our field!" Little Jack shouted.
"And there is my tree!" shouted Billy. His anxious parents
came out to meet him.

Little Jack Rabbit escorted Little Charlie Mole home. Father Mole was clearing a path to the door. He was not pleased with either of them.

But Mother Mole fussed over Little Charlie and told him to go and sit by the fire until his feet were quite dry.

Little Jack's parents were talking to the old hare. Little Jack bounded toward them. His mother hugged him.

His father said "Thank you" and "Good-bye" to the old hare.

Winter passed into spring. Green leaves and catkins hung in the hedges. Flowers opened. Birds built nests.

Little Jack Rabbit and his friends were given permission to go again to the cabbage field. Little Jack had to take his sisters along. Little Charlie was told to be home before supper.

They came to the cabbage field . . . BUT THERE WERE NO CABBAGES!

The field was plowed and showed the first green shoots of corn.

But there stood the scarecrow! And how smart he looked with new gloves and a new hat too, which the crows had decorated with feathers.

The scarecrow saw all the little animals at the edge of the field, and he waved his scarf and his hands excitedly.

"There is our friend!" shouted Little Jack.

They raced to the scarecrow. Billy Squirrel got there first and was so brave he jumped up onto the scarecrow's arm.

The others gathered around, and Little Jack made the necessary introductions.

The scarecrow beamed down on them, a huge smile across his face. His heart was filled with joy, and he was lonely no more.